Silent F… …es

Heather Lea

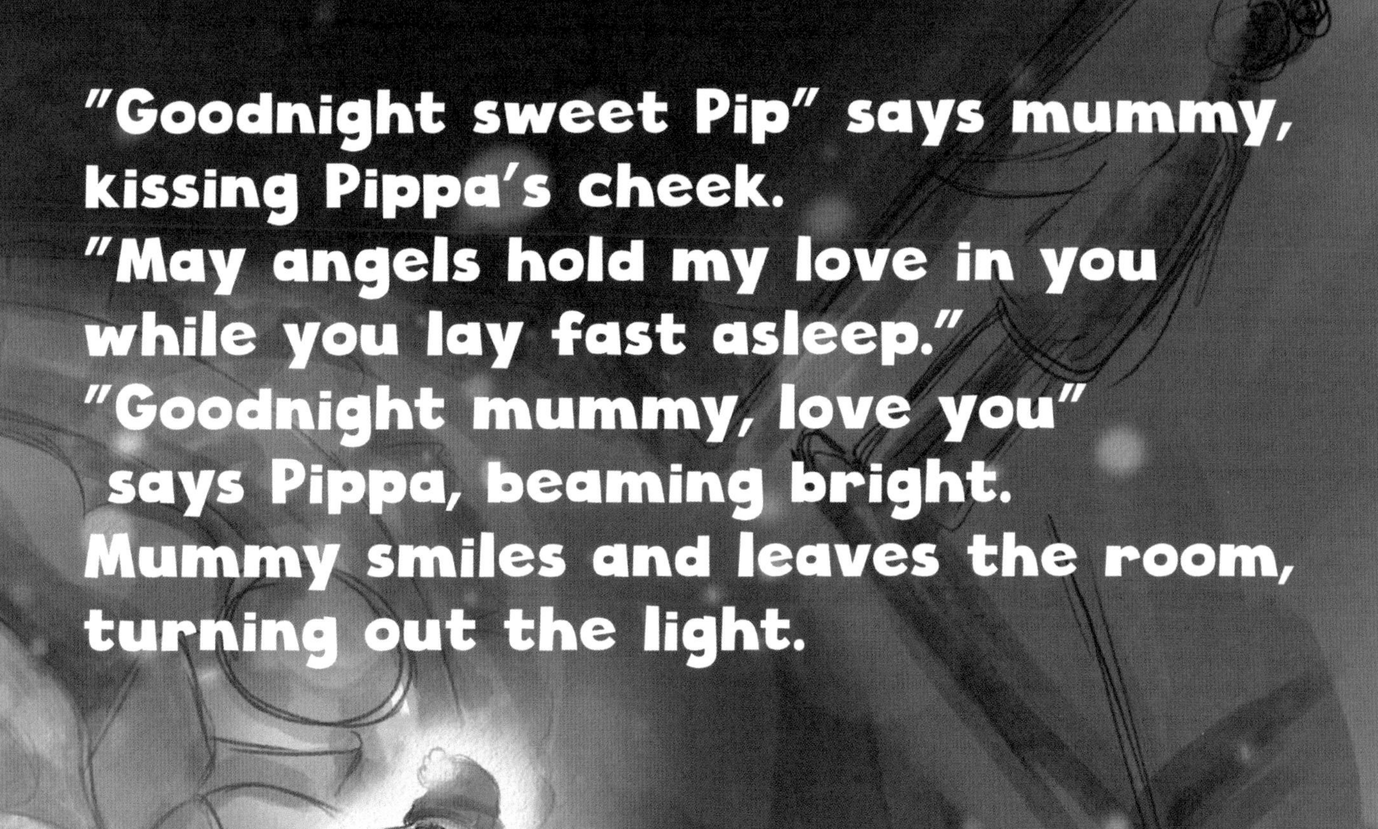

"Goodnight sweet Pip" says mummy,
kissing Pippa's cheek.
"May angels hold my love in you
while you lay fast asleep."
"Goodnight mummy, love you"
says Pippa, beaming bright.
Mummy smiles and leaves the room,
turning out the light.

Pippa loves her bedtime,
the darkness of the night.
She snuggles under blankets,
holds her teddy tight.
Laying in her cosy bed,
she closes eyes so tight,
Lets out a sigh,
tells ted "goodnight",
gets settled for the night.

Outside, the moon's beam
shines so bright but clouds dance
in that truth.
The sky is bruised in colour;
speckled red in black and blue.
The stars are glazed with misty
hue but twinkle down with love.
All seems very silent
in the darkened skies above.

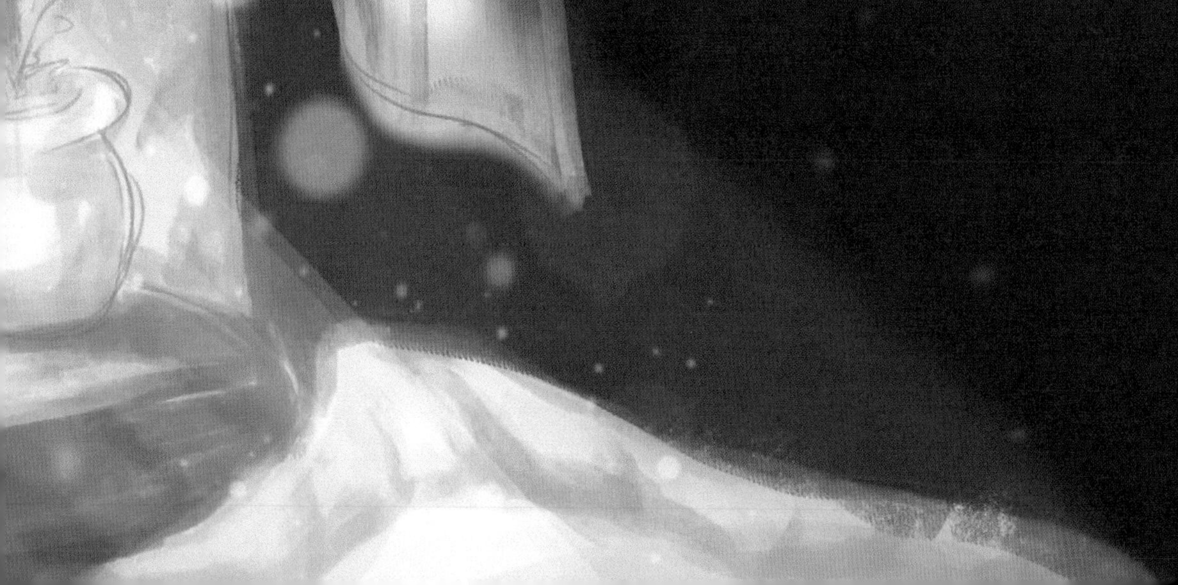

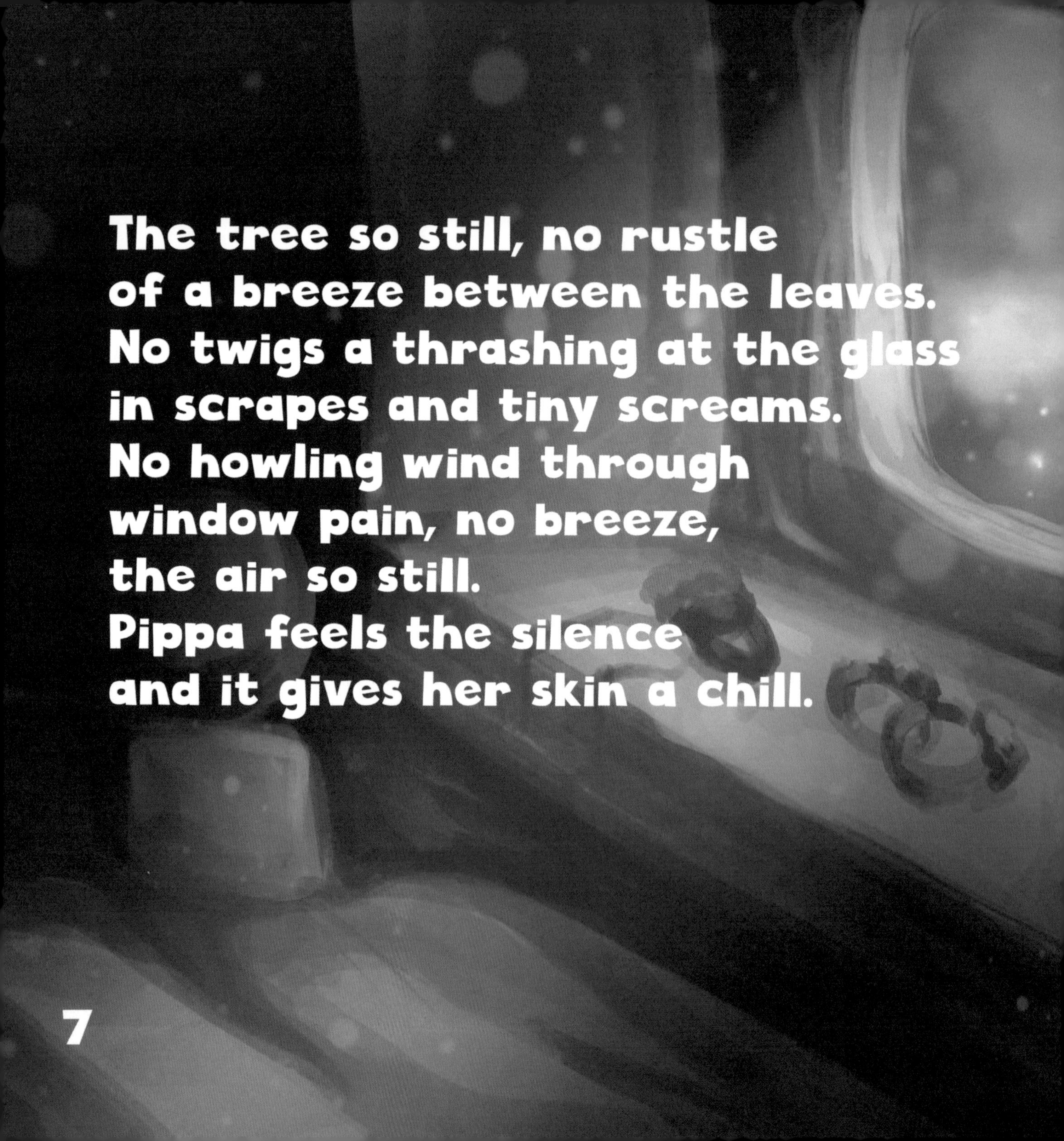

The tree so still, no rustle
of a breeze between the leaves.
No twigs a thrashing at the glass
in scrapes and tiny screams.
No howling wind through
window pain, no breeze,
the air so still.
Pippa feels the silence
and it gives her skin a chill.

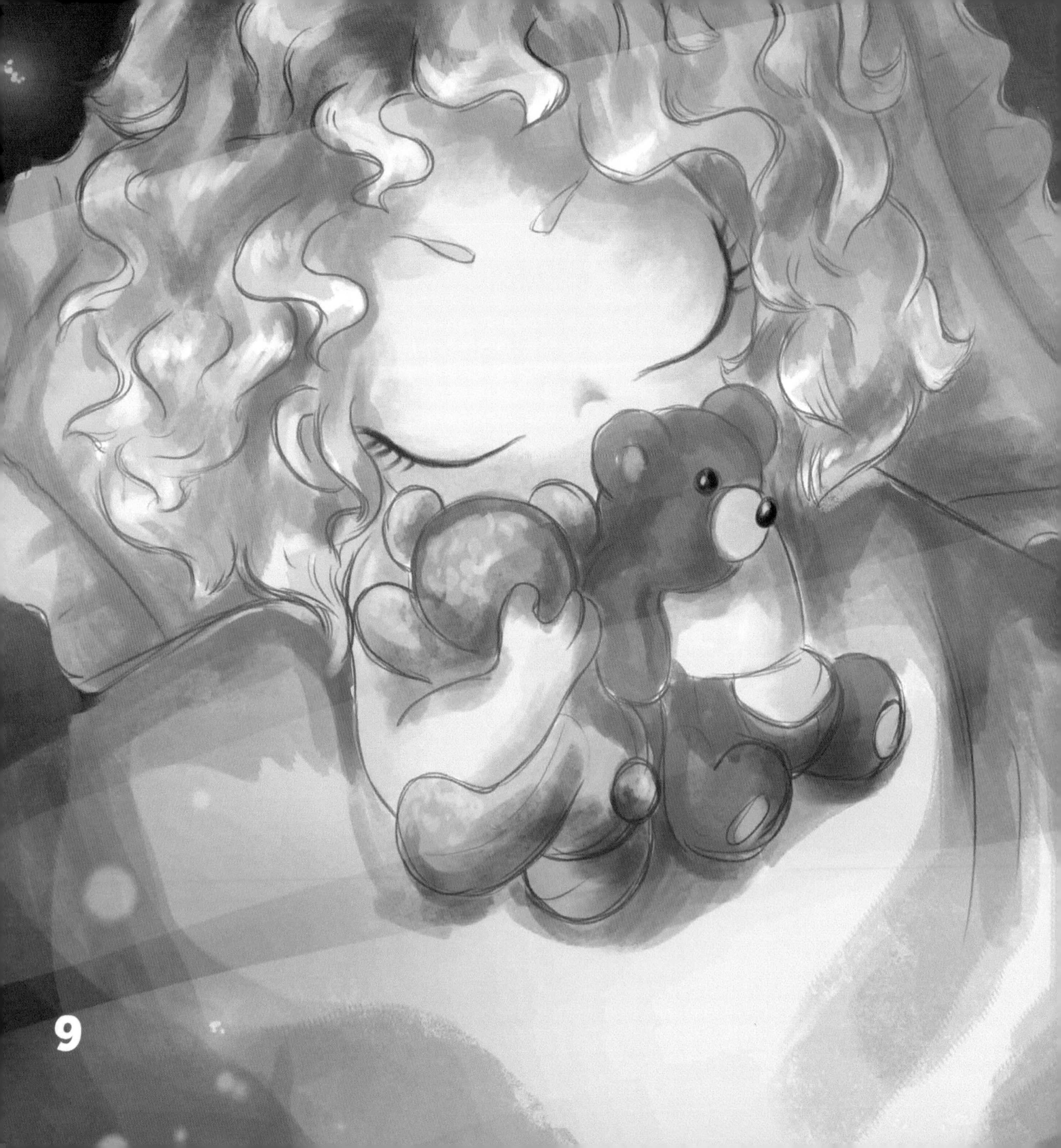

She squeezes eyes so tightly
in the silence of the night,
Then grabs another teddy bear,
holds both teddies tight.
Her mind is dancing with a fear
of everything around.
The silence grabs her troubles,
she craves to hear a sound.

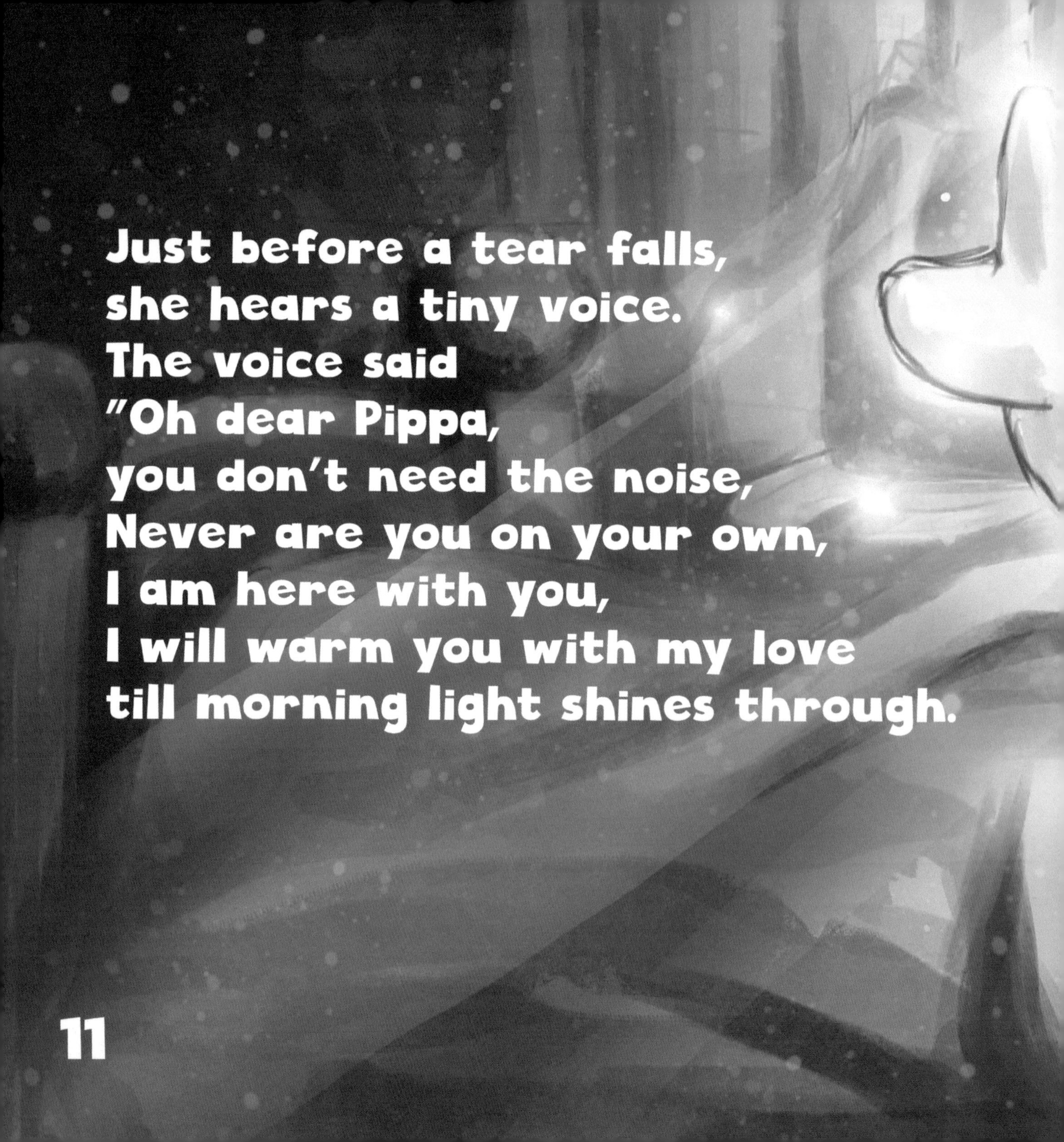

Just before a tear falls,
she hears a tiny voice.
The voice said
"Oh dear Pippa,
you don't need the noise,
Never are you on your own,
I am here with you,
I will warm you with my love
till morning light shines through.

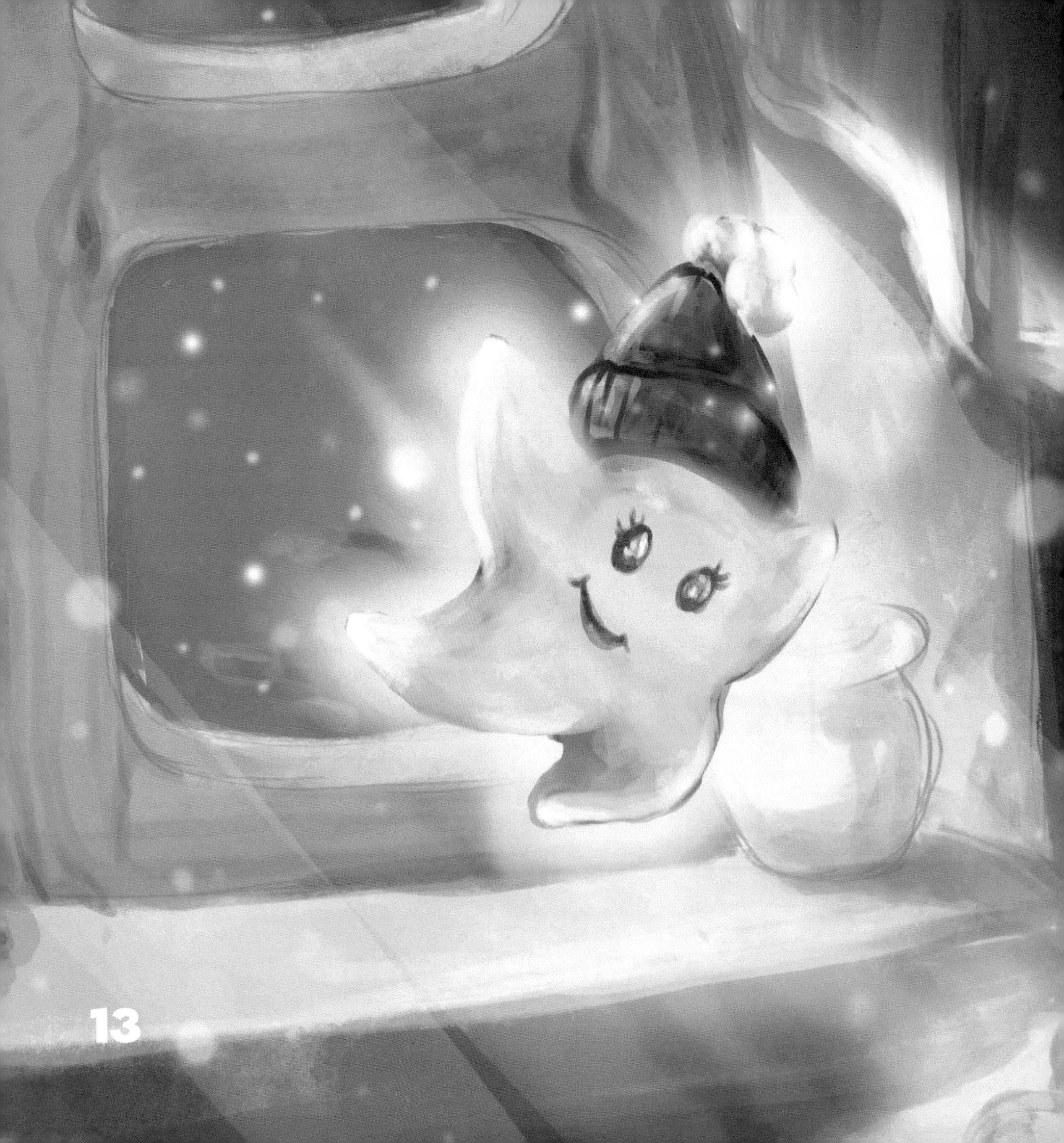

Dear Pippa, in this silence,
listen to your heart.
Let your music sing to you and
feel your dreaming start"
Pippa doesn't fear the voice,
it calms her with the tone.
Pippa feels a warmth that stops
the feeling of alone.

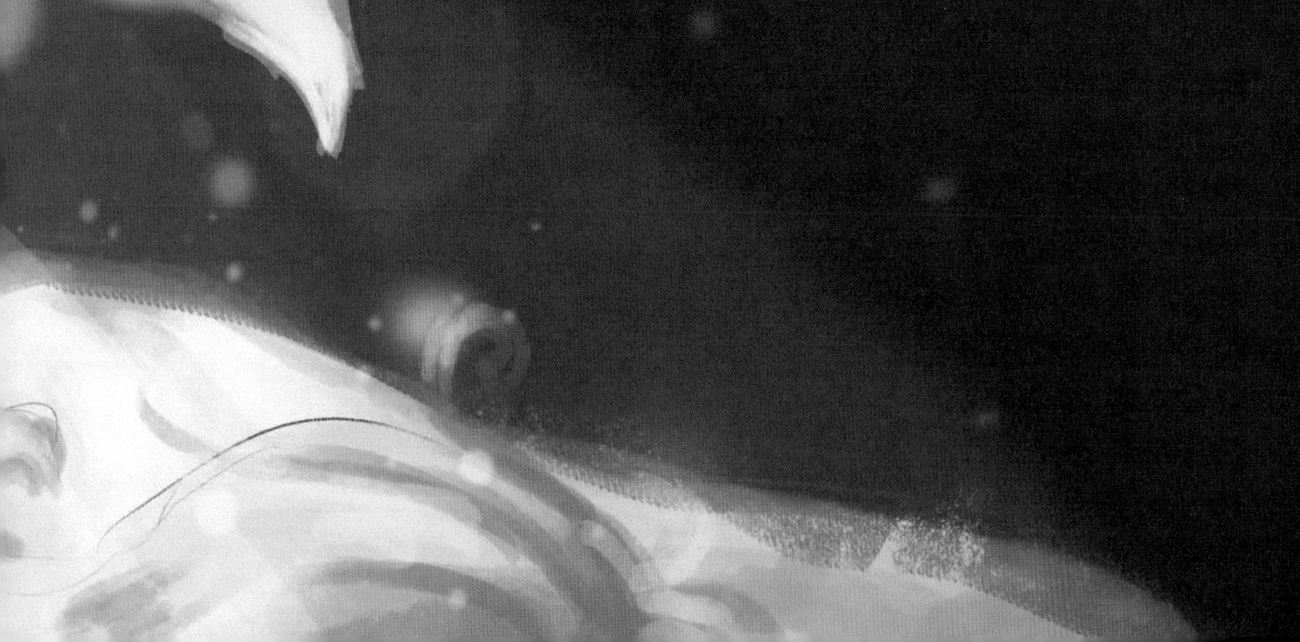

She breathes in deep,
breathes out so slow,
then breathes in once again,
Allows each fear
to wash away,
like teardrops in the rain.
Before long she is
fast asleep,
adrift in lands of love,
Resting for this night
right now but floating
high above.

Passing through the clouds
of thought,
she hears a friendly voice,
It echoes through her memory,
like a feather-fluttered noise.
It fills her with a feeling
that makes her think of home,
Like everything is love
and she could never feel alone.

"I am your soul, sweet Pippa,
forever at your call.
I will catch you with my love
if ever you do fall.
Take this love and hold it,
whenever you feel sad
Let me be the best friend
that you have ever had"

The Twitter
of the fluttered birds,
the morning lights the room.
The sun shines down with pride
after nodding to the moon.
Pippa wakes from slumberland,
arises to the bright
Full of joy and happiness,
not a fear in sight.

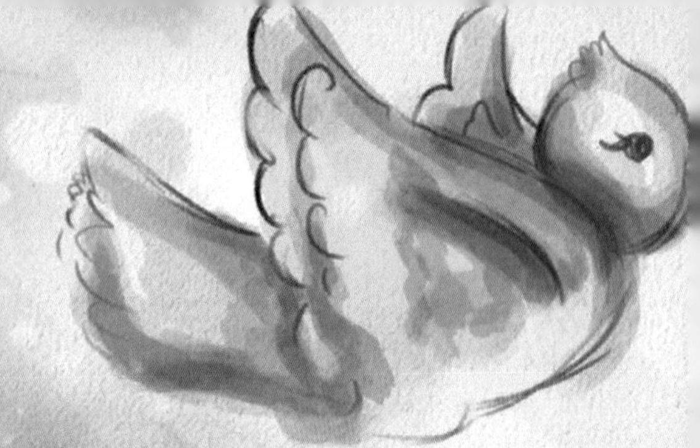

Pippa can't remember
the dream she had that night,
All she can remember is
a loving, glowing light.
Forever she will hold
that feeling,
unknowing of the why,
But truth be known dear Pippa
had found her wings to fly.

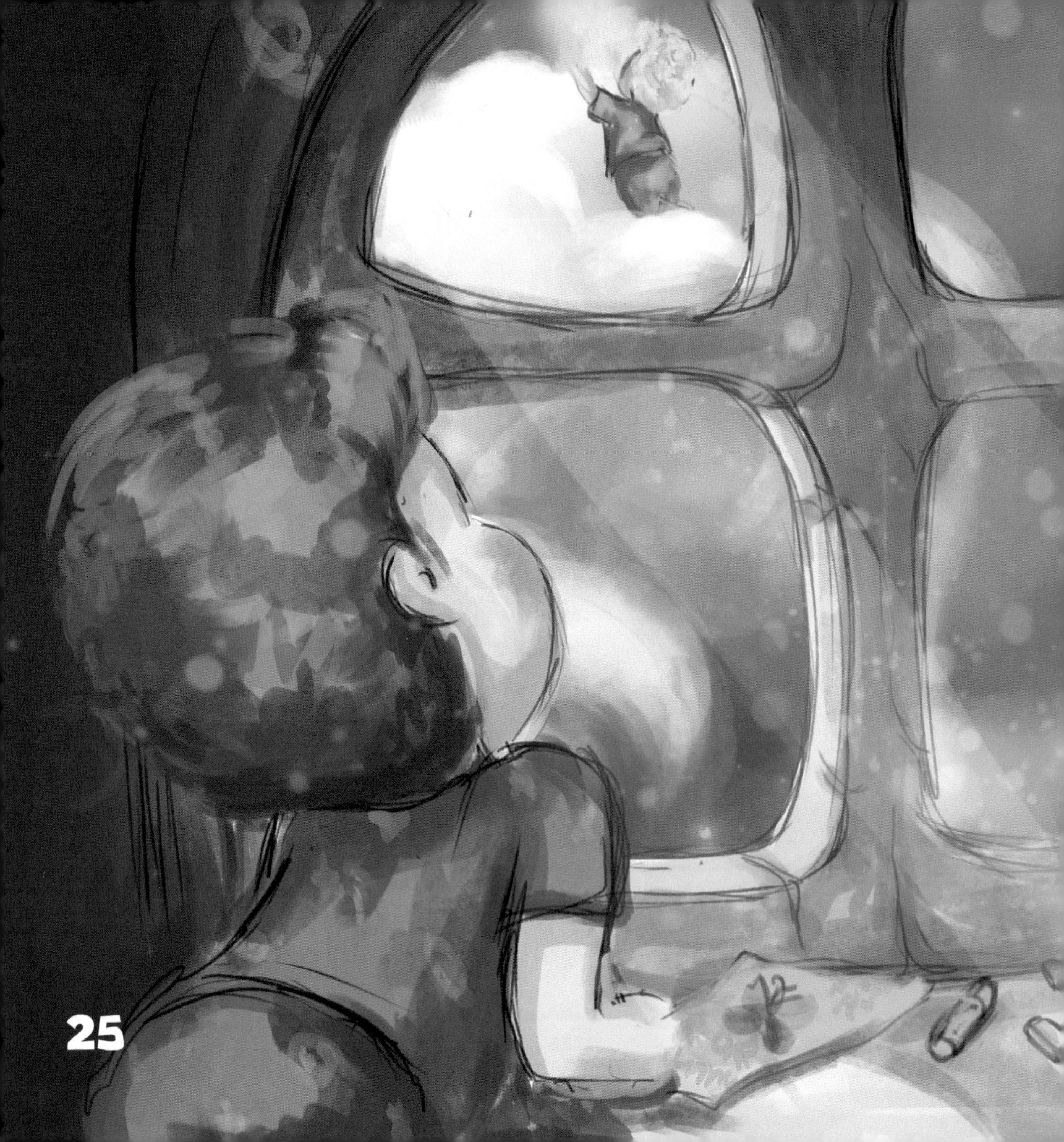

Maybe you too fear the dark
when mummy takes the light.
Maybe you too think
of silent worries in the night,
But maybe you, like Pip,
just need to drift up high
And maybe you will
too find your wings
and learn to fly.

Shine bright,
Little star,
Shine bright
For all you are.
Shine bright
Little light
Shine bright
Into the night.

Printed in Great Britain
by Amazon